Mystery of the Golden Palomino

The Dallas O'Neil Mysteries

MYSTERY OF THE GOLDEN PALOMINO

by

JERRY B. JENKINS

MOODY PRESS

CHICAGO

This Guideposts edition is published by special
arrangement with Moody Press

A NOTE TO THE READER

This book was selected by the same
editors who prepare *Guideposts*, a
monthly magazine filled with true stories of people's adventures in faith.

If you have found inspiration in this
book, we think you'll find monthly
help and inspiration in the exciting
stories that appear in our magazine.
Guideposts is not sold on the news-
stand. It's available by subscription
only. And subscribing is easy. All you
have to do is write Guideposts Asso-
ciates, Inc., 39 Seminary Hill Road,
Carmel, New York 10512. For those
with special reading needs, *Guideposts*
is published in Big Print, Braille, and
Talking Magazine.

When you subscribe, each month
you can count on receiving exciting
new evidence of God's presence and
His abiding love for His people.

©1989 by
JERRY B. JENKINS

ISBN: 0-8024-8386-0

4 5 6 Printing/LC/Year 93 92 91

Printed in the United States of America

To Michael

Contents

1

Jimmy's Dream

Jimmy Calabresi was the only kid I ever knew who had reins on his bike. I'm serious. He had rigged a beautiful set of reins for a horse, mouth bit and all, on his handlebars.

He set the bit over the center post and wrapped the leather straps around enough times so they wouldn't get caught in the spokes of his front wheel. He put saddle bags, real leather ones, on the back fender. I know if he had figured a way to do it, he would have thrown a blanket over the seat and topped it with a saddle. He had one. In fact, he had all the stuff you need for a horse. Except a horse. That was his dream.

Jimmy always mounted his bike by running alongside it and hopping on, and he made clicking noises with his tongue to get his rolling steed going. He pasted plastic letters on the back fender that spelled "Star Diamond."

The funny thing was—and this *was* funny, even though I never told him so or teased him about it the way the other guys did—Jimmy's imaginary horse, Star Diamond, wasn't limited to his bike. He's my best friend—Jimmy, that is, not the horse —so I ought to know. Jimmy would leave his house riding that horse, just sort of cantering along with his hands on his imaginary reins, until he reached his bike.

Then he would wrap the reins around his hands, only until he had hopped aboard and got up enough speed. Then he would ride no-handed, except that he would use the reins to steer. He flopped over a couple of times until he got used to the reins, but he did pretty well when he was going fast enough. He could make long, gradual turns around curves, even while swatting the back of his horse with the leftover reins.

When he parked his bike, no matter where, he padlocked it and wrapped the reins around a post, just like you would tie up a horse. That got him razzed the most, especially by our friends in the Baker Street Sports Club. I mean, here it was, baseball season, and Calabresi, our catcher, had an imaginary horse. He'd tie it up outside our shed, where we held our meetings, or even to the backstop at our ball field on Mrs. Ferguson's acreage.

No matter how much red-headed Cory, or Bugsy (our little black friend), or Toby, our lumbering third-baseman, made fun of him, Jimmy never quit pretending he was riding that horse. For some reason, even after he tied up Star Diamond, we would see him pretending to ride to his position behind home plate or onto the bench. During the school year I had even seen him sort of privately pretend to be riding in the halls between classes. He had it bad.

Not only did Jimmy have all that horse stuff, but he also had a stable. That had been on his property for years, long before he and his family had moved in—and that was longer ago than I can remember. Two years ago he asked me to help him build a stable "just in case."

"Just in case of what?" I asked.

"In case I finally get my horse."

"What are your chances?"

He shook his head. "No better than ever, but I've been wishing and hoping and praying more."

By now his horse book, as I liked to call it, was well worn. It was a large, slim volume about Nellie, a poor little country girl who longs for a horse for more than a year. Then she gets sick, and it looks like she might die. She dreams about a big, mahogany brown stallion. Her parents can't afford it, but as she lies deathly ill, her neighbors gather all their money and present the family with the horse of her dreams.

Jimmy wouldn't even let me borrow *A Horse for Nellie*. I could read it only when I was at his house. I admit it made me cry, and I couldn't wait to get back there to read another chapter. Finally I was allowed to stay overnight, and I stayed up late to finish it.

Of course, in the end the horse is so beautiful and Nellie is so thrilled that she soon recovers from whatever it was that was supposed to kill her, and the book ends with her riding all over the countryside on Mahogany, with no saddle, her arms wrapped around the great horse's neck.

I could see why Jimmy wanted a horse so badly after reading that book. In fact, one of the reasons I never teased Jimmy about pretending to have a horse was that I had had one once. It broke my heart when my dad had to sell Lightning to help pay to put my grandma in a nursing home. But I understood. I really did. There were many things we had to go without as long as grandma was in that home, and my horse was one of them.

There were times when I pretended Lightning was still around. He was a beautiful white horse, and it took me a long time to get over not having him anymore. Most of the other guys thought pretending you had a horse or a little friend was for babies or sissies, and that's why they let Jimmy have it every time he came galloping up, or riding his bike horse, or steering his way around corners indoors with imaginary reins in his hands.

"Hey, Calabresi," Cory would bellow, his orange mop flopping, "when you gonna grow up? If you're gonna pretend, why don't you pretend you've got a girl friend?" Bugsy would cackle, and Toby would double over.

Jimmy might purse his lips or even scowl, but he never answered. He'd tell me privately, "I used to just hope and wish and wish and hope, but since I became a Christian I've been praying about this."

I had to be careful how I answered him. I knew that Jimmy's dream of having a horse might not be the most important thing on God's mind, but I didn't want to discourage him either. "What kind of a horse are you praying for?"

"You know," he said.

It was true. I knew. All he'd ever talked about was his golden palomino. He'd written and even talked about it in reports at school. In fact, one of our teachers told him that "golden palomino" is redundant.

"Redundant! What's that?" he asked.

"They mean the same," the teacher explained. "Just about the only horse that could be golden is a palomino. The word means pale, and palominos have tan or cream-colored bodies and white or very light manes and tails."

"But mine's going to be very yellow, very golden," Jimmy would say, looking off into the distance.

I knew he could just see that horse. I could see Lightning when I thought hard enough about him.

Helping Jimmy build that corral was one of the hardest things I had ever done. His father wouldn't help, not because he was being mean but because he didn't want Jimmy to get his hopes up.

"It isn't that I couldn't afford a horse, J.C.," his father said more than once. "It's just that if you won't settle for anything less than a yellow palomino, you're talking about a thoroughbred Arabian, and I can't even come close to that. Anyway, you buy the feed yourself, you muck the stall yourself, you buy the leather goods yourself, you build the corral yourself, and you take care of the animal all by yourself. Otherwise, no way."

Jimmy was so excited that for a long time he took that as an answer. He thought his dad would buy him the animal if Jimmy agreed to everything. Of course he agreed, but his father had really been simply trying to talk him out of it. His parents always used to say, "You'll grow out of it, and better that you do that before you have the horse than after."

Even that didn't discourage him. Once we had that crazy corral built, he pranced around inside it as if he already had a horse. That was one time when I really felt sorry for him and wondered if his parents had any idea how much this horse meant to him.

I had dinner with him that night and heard the disappointing news. His father didn't seem to care that much.

"I'm impressed that you got all that work done, J. C., but I gotta tell ya, I made no promises about a horse, and I'm not inclined to get you one."

"But why?"

"I'm not inclined to discuss it in front of company either," his father said, making me turn red. "Why don't you just keep pretending? That's been good enough up till now."

Jimmy was so angry he looked as if he might burst into tears. "Dad!" he said, then excused himself and ran from the room.

I could tell his father wanted to make him come back, but he didn't want a scene in front of me, so we just finished our meal awkward and silent.

After dinner Mr. Calabresi did something that really made me feel uncomfortable. He took me aside and talked about his son in a way that I knew I was not supposed to tell Jimmy. But we were best friends. I wouldn't tell him, of course, but it was hard.

For one thing, until now I had never heard Mr. Calabresi call Jimmy anything but J. C.

"What James doesn't realize—of course, how could he know?—is that I just might be able to do something about that horse dream of his, maybe even soon."

"Really?"

Mr. Calabresi nodded. "I know you don't know anything about my business," he said, "but you know I'm a salesman."

"Sure."

"Well, every once in a while, we salesmen get chances for big deals. We get paid on commission. You know what that means?"

"Sort of. I think."

"It means that we get a salary just like everybody else— well, maybe a little less than most—but we get part of each sale to make up the rest of our pay."

"I know you've done well," I said. "Jimmy likes to brag about it, and nobody blames him. He has lots of nice stuff, and you have a great place here."

"We do all right, but you know a horse like he wants isn't just a few hundred dollars. I mean, if I could put a little aside for a while, get him to chip in some of his own money, and find a decent nag for say four or five hundred bucks, I'd do it in a minute. But one time I took him horse shopping, and he made me mad."

"I know. He told me about it. He feels terrible about it."

"He ought to. He acted real ungrateful that day."

"He didn't mean to."

"I know he didn't mean to, but he was sure obnoxious. He just flat didn't want anything but a yellow or golden horse. I saw some beautiful black and brown ones, even a speckled gray one that was gorgeous. He turned up his nose at every one. Dallas, there was a chestnut brown mare that had such a shiny, healthy looking coat that I almost bought it for myself."

"Don't you think if you had bought it for Jimmy he would have grown to like it?"

Mr. Calabresi shrugged. "I wasn't going to force it on him. Anyway, the deal was that he was supposed to come up with a hundred of the money himself. He insisted that he didn't want to waste his money on anything but the horse he wanted."

"A golden palomino."

"Exactly."

"Is there one around?"

"Oh, you can get 'em. There are horse brokers who deal with Arabians and part Arabians. I could afford a mixed breed, but still it'd be a lot more than a few hundred."

"And you're going to do that this summer?"

"Maybe. I've got a major proposal being looked at by a large company right now. If they make the purchase from me, my commission will be more than enough for James's horse. We'll also be able to pay off our car and add that room we've always wanted."

"Wow."

Mrs. Calabresi scowled, and Mr. Calabresi looked suddenly nervous. "Well," he said, "that's confidential, private, family business. I shouldn't have told you all that, and I'd appreciate it if you wouldn't share it with anyone."

"Oh, I won't," I promised.

"Especially with James."

"No, sir."

"OK?"

I nodded. But, like I said, it wasn't easy.

2

The Pitch

Jimmy looked pretty funny riding his bike to baseball practice. He came around the turn in Mrs. Ferguson's long driveway with a shin guard sticking out of each saddle bag and a satchel hanging from the seat, in which he carried his helmet, catcher's mask, and rolled-up chest protector. He had fastened his bat to the handlebars with his extra length of reins and still had enough left over to steer the bike.

Because he had enough speed, Jimmy was able to shift the reins to the proper grip for horseback riding, neatly held between his fingers. He rode that way so much that he had actually developed calluses between his fingers. "That'll help me when I get my horse," he'd say. "There won't be any getting used to the reins."

When the guys in the Baker Street Sports Club saw him, they yelled and waved. When he tried to wave back, his bicycle/horse weaved a little to the right, and he headed for the gently curved edge of Mrs. Ferguson's crushed stone drive. He had learned long ago not to try to straighten out a bike, especially with leather reins, too quickly.

He gently and gradually re-gripped the reins and let the bike slide off the side of the driveway onto the grass. As we watched in amazement, Jimmy repositioned himself on the bike and pedaled harder, looking as if he was urging his horse on. He had made it look like he had steered Star Diamond off the driveway and onto the grass, then over to the backstop. As he slowed he deftly put the ends of the reins on the handlebars and guided the bike to the backstop, where he slipped off and wrapped the leather around the post.

"Why don't you let the horse catch?" Cory called from second base.

Toby came in from third base, following big Jack Bastable, who loped in from first. "Is your horse hungry, Calabresi?" Toby jeered.

"What's his name again?" Jack asked, dead serious.

"Star Diamond."

Jack reached out and patted the front fender. "Whoa, boy," he said, eyes wide with the wonder of his imagination, mental retardation stalling it at the level of a much younger child. "Here's some oats and sugar."

Jack reached an open palm in front of the fender and pantomimed feeding the bike a handful of goodies.

Toby shook his head and stared at Jimmy. "You're about the same level as Jack," he said.

I looked at him sharply. One rule we had in the Baker Street Sports Club was that no one was to make fun of Jack or refer to him as retarded or stupid or anything like that. I didn't want to make an issue of it right then, because it was clear from the look on his face that Jack had no idea what had been said.

Jimmy understood perfectly, of course. It was the same old story. Everybody thought Jimmy should give up pretending, grow up, give up his dream. He didn't appear to let it bother him. He didn't smile, but he didn't scowl either. He just sat on the ground and put on his equipment.

"Have you hit yet?" he asked Toby.

"Nope."

"Let's see if you can hit like you can talk."

That sounded like a good idea to me too. I was in charge of who hit when, so I told Toby, "Yeah, get a helmet on."

When he moved to the plate, Jimmy trotted out to me. "Let me call the pitches," he said.

"I usually do," I reminded him. "No bean balls."

"I wouldn't do that," he said. "Don't need to with big-mouth-little-stick Toby."

I fought a smile. I didn't want to encourage bad feelings between teammates, but Toby deserved something for the way he had treated Jimmy.

I rubbed up the ball, trying to separate the covering from the inside, at least around the seams, so I could get a better grip. Jimmy squatted behind the plate, and Toby stepped in. I studied Jimmy, looking for a sign. He shot down his index finger, then touched the inside of his thigh with the backs of his fingers. Fastball inside to the target.

Jimmy settled in with the glove set up about waist high on the hitter, splitting the plate.

I went into a slow wind-up, knowing that the target was fake. It was meant for Toby in case he glanced back or was able to see out of the corner of his eye. He might have guessed fastball, and he certainly would have guessed waist high and right down the middle.

At the last instant, when Toby was totally focused on me, Jimmy shifted without a sound and moved the target higher and farther inside. In fact, the pitch, if I threw it where he called for it, would have been a ball, high and inside. I hoped I had enough control not to let it get away from me. Jimmy didn't want me to hit Toby any more than I wanted to hit him, but he did want a pitch high and tight, maybe right in under his elbow.

It's hard for a big hitter to get much bat on the ball if he can't extend his arms. If that pitch went where it was supposed to, Toby would not be extending his arms.

I let it fly.

The ball started just above waist level and sailed up and in, right to the glove. It looked tempting to Toby, and he stepped and swung, but the ball was in under his hands. He smacked his bat on the ground and stepped back in, digging with his back foot for more traction and leverage.

Jimmy called for the same pitch, same location, but made a fist after the signal, indicating that I should take something off it.

I gripped the ball deep in my palm, wrapping all four fingers around it, then threw it with the same motion in the same place. By the time it left my hand, Toby had already decided it was the same pitch, stepped a little shorter and a little more to his left, and prepared to pull it to left.

He swung way too early, almost lost his balance, and had to hop and skip to keep from sprawling in the dirt. I heard Jimmy mutter something and Toby say something back.

"What'd you say?" I asked.

Toby was practice swinging. "The cowboy here says I'm history," he said. "I told him he didn't dare call for either of those pitches again."

He was right. Jimmy called for a fastball just off the outside corner. He set up inside, his glove high, right where the first two pitches had gone. I was a little surprised he hadn't called for a curve, but we had agreed that neither Cory nor I would throw many curves until we were older. We both knew how, but we also knew it wasn't good for our arms.

I was sure that if I threw a sweeping curve that looked as if we were coming back inside, but which slid out across the outside corner, we'd have a pitch Toby couldn't reach. But Jimmy's call wasn't bad either. He was asking for a hard fastball, too close to take, but far enough from the first two pitches that Toby would not likely be ready for it.

We got lucky. I threw the pitch very hard and very outside. Toby had somehow guessed what we were up to, and he nearly stepped on the plate, setting himself to be able to reach a strike on the outside corner. The problem was, the pitch was so far off the corner that he held up. I was sure glad I hadn't come close to the corner like Jimmy wanted, or Toby would have put it in the creek. He was that kind of a hitter.

He laughed and chortled about our "amateur tricks," and Jimmy trotted out to me, mad. "I don't know what to call now, but you gotta throw something he can't hit."

"Well, what do you think we've set him up for?"

"I don't know. I'm just afraid that if he guesses, he'll have the last laugh."

"Well, let's try a fake change in the dirt. He's always been a sucker for a low pitch, and I'll see how much I can get it to dance. If he can hit this pitch, he deserves the last laugh."

Jimmy was encouraged and hurried back to the plate.

Bugsy was catcalling from shortstop. "Hey, I thought this was batting practice! Candy pitches! You guys are callin' pitches and everything. Just throw it in there, straight and three-quarter speed, just like for anybody else!"

Toby stopped him. "No! It's all right! They're tryin' to strike me out, but they can't! And soon as I get a hit, I get the next ride on Star Diamond, right, J. C.?"

He said the J. C. with such derision that he really made Jimmy mad. I could see Jimmy tensing up, furious that anyone would use his dad's nickname for him. He pounded his glove and, without saying anything, encouraged me to blow it past Toby.

I toed the rubber, and Jimmy hollered, "Give 'im smoke, right down the middle. He can't touch you!"

"You wouldn't dare!" Toby said, bat back.

Jimmy didn't flash a sign. I had to wonder if he was so mad he was really calling for a fastball down the middle. I had learned to seldom throw anything down the middle, even if I was hot and thought I could get it past a hitter. That's dangerous. That's home-run pitching.

Or was this just a game? He wanted Toby to think that was what we were going to do, or at least to wonder? The problem was, Toby's ridicule made me want to try that too. I was just proud enough to want to prove to him that he couldn't hit my best fastball, even if it was right down the middle and he knew—or thought he knew—it was coming.

I waited, looking, studying to see if there was any clue as to what I should do or what Jimmy really wanted.

Two clues came at once. Jimmy set the target right down the middle and waist high again, which he wouldn't have done so early if that was what he really wanted. And he also hollered, "Just like we said, Dal! Right down the pipe!"

That wasn't what we had said, so he must be wanting what we had discussed—the moving fastball in the dirt. Meanwhile, Toby was still down on the end of the bat. Usually, with two strikes, he would shorten up a little and just try to get the bat on the ball. To me this meant he really thought he knew what was coming. He was guessing either straight fastball or straight change. I didn't know how he could hit one while guessing the other, but that was *his* problem.

I went into a high kick, faked like I was slowing everything for a big change-up, then finished fast with a hard pitch below his knees that had everything on it I could muster. He was fooled, but he's always had fast hands. He had settled back on his heels when he thought he would be waiting out a change of pace, but when the fastball came in, looking tantalizingly strike-like, he reacted quickly.

He stepped and began his swing, only to see the ball dart down. Toby hatcheted at it and got a piece of it. The ball slammed onto the plate and bounced high back over Jimmy's head. We all smiled, and Toby hooted. "Ooh, pretty good, boys! Made me swing at a bad pitch, huh? But I'm still alive!

"Oh and two," Jimmy said, just loud enough for everyone to hear.

"Let me pitch!" Cory yelled.

"No! Me!" Bugsy said.

"Not me!" Jack said earnestly, hands on his knees near first, and we all laughed.

Jimmy squatted and called for a fastball inside at the knees. If I couldn't throw that pitch, I didn't belong on the mound. It was a good, solid call. The question was, could Toby get his bat on it? Jimmy set up outside, then drifted in as I wound and fired.

3

The Razz

Toby swung right through the ball for strike three. Jimmy whooped and hollered, and Toby threw his bat away in mock disgust. He wasn't really mad, but I knew he would be if Jimmy didn't back off a little.

"All right," I said, "get back in there for regular batting practice."

"Strike him out again, Dal!" Jimmy shouted as Toby retrieved his bat and stepped back in.

He started flashing signs for fastballs and change-ups and even a curve. I ignored him and threw three-quarter speed letter-high fastballs in Toby's wheelhouse, well out over the plate, fat, candy, home-run pitches he turned on and drove deep toward the creek. Three, four, five in a row sailed above the outfielders' heads.

"Next hitter," I said.

Cory jogged in. "You gonna try to strike me out first, too, hotshot?" he asked, grinning.

"He could," Jimmy growled.

"No way," Cory said, jamming a helmet down over his red hair. "Remember I haven't struck out this year."

"That's 'cause you haven't faced Dallas," Jimmy said. He hollered out to me, "What do you say, Dal? How 'bout lettin' everybody have one live at bat against you before they get their BP swings?"

I shrugged. Frankly, I didn't think I could strike out Cory. He had developed into the best contact hitter on the team, and even though he wasn't as fast as Bugsy or me or some of the littler guys, he had earned the lead-off spot. He got on base so often with walks and hits that we needed him to start games that way.

"It'll be good for you, too, Dal," Jimmy said. "You don't get that much real, live pitching action between games."

I shrugged again. That made sense. "Yeah, but I don't know about trying to strike everybody out. That's not what I do in the games. I'd rather force them into groundouts or popouts. That's a lot better for my arm."

Jimmy started to nod, but Cory would have none of it. "You can try to get the rest of these rummies to ground out or pop out. I wanna see if you can strike me out."

"He can," Jimmy said.

I wasn't so sure.

"No way, cowboy," Cory said. "He strikes me out, I'll never say another word about your toy horse."

I could see Jimmy's shoulders sag. He was tired of all the hassle, just because he pretended to have a horse. I wasn't sure Cory could keep his end of the bargain, even if I did strike him out, but worse, I didn't see a weakness in Cory's hitting. I knew he could reach a rising fastball, but I hadn't seen him even go after one since the second game of the season. He swung and missed a first pitch that was up and out of the strike zone, but the pitcher couldn't get him to chase anything else, and he walked.

Maybe the challenge of striking out a pure contact hitter like Cory would be good for me. And it wouldn't bother me that much if I couldn't do it. But if I failed, would that open the door to merciless teasing of Jimmy about Star Diamond?

"C'mon, O'Neil," Jimmy wailed. "Strike out this bush leaguer!"

I peered in for the sign. Jimmy called for a fastball on the outside corner, about letter high. I shook it off. If it was a strike, Cory could hit it. If it wasn't, we were immediately behind in the count, because he wouldn't chase a bad pitch. Jimmy ran through the signs again and called for the same pitch. I pursed my lips and shook it off more vigorously. He ran out to the mound.

Before he could say anything, I said, "C'mon, Jim, we're wasting time. I can't pitch every guy like it's the last out of the World Series. A lot of guys have to hit yet. Anyway, he can hit the high fastball on the outside corner."

"Yeah, but he's not expecting it. Just throw the pitch I call for. I want this strikeout more than you do, so let me handle it."

"You gonna throw the pitch, too?"

Jimmy ignored me and went back behind the plate. He called for the same pitch.

I wound and fired. It was perfect, just where Jimmy wanted it.

Cory checked his swing.

Jimmy shrieked, "Strike one!"

"No! No way!" Cory said. "Outside and high! Not even close! Ball one!"

"Wait a minute," Bugsy said. "Hitter can't call it."

"Well, the catcher can't either!" Cory said.

"Who better than the catcher?" Bugsy said.

"The pitcher then!" Jimmy said.

All eyes turned to me.

"I thought it was in there," I said, "but how can I call it?"

Jimmy cheered, Cory argued, and Bugsy shouted, "That's good enough for me. Strike one, Cory!"

Cory shook his head and stepped back in.

I couldn't believe my eyes. Jimmy was calling for the same pitch. I thought that was crazy, but I wasn't in the mood for any more arguing. I didn't even nod. I just wound up and threw the ball to the same spot, same speed.

Cory stepped and cracked the ball deep between right and center. It bounced to the edge of the creek and took two relay throws to get back to me.

Everyone was silent, even Cory. Jimmy just sat there.

Finally, Cory spoke. "I thought you were gonna try to strike me out before you started in with the candy pitches."

He knew that was no easy pitch. So did Jimmy. So did anybody who saw it.

"That was my fault," Jimmy said. "If I'da called inside and low, it'd be strike two."

"It'd be ball one!" Cory said. "If it'd been hittable on the inside I would have taken it to left."

"Not a chance," Jimmy said. "You hit an outside pitch to right center. If you could have just as easily hit an inside pitch to left, you're the best hitter in history."

"You said it. Not me."

That made me mad. Jimmy was right. Nobody can protect the whole plate. You have to guess a little. I wanted another chance at Cory, but I didn't want to admit it. I was glad when Jimmy suggested it.

"Don't s'pose you'd give us another chance. Same deal?"

"Bring it on!" Cory said. "But unless you strike me out, I can say what I want about your two-wheeled pony!"

The other guys complained. "Let's quit all this wasting time! We want to hit too!"

Cory calmed them by promising that he would give Jimmy and me one more at bat to try to strike him out, and that would be his BP for the day.

"Fair enough," Bugsy said. "Get on with it. In fact, strike him out, Dal."

I wanted to.

Jimmy called for a low change-up. A great idea. It sailed on me, came in high, Cory laid off it. Ball one. He chortled. I seethed.

Jimmy wanted a fastball just off the outside corner at the knees. I liked that call too. It was about two inches outside, but because Cory had had luck driving an outside pitch for what would have been at least a double, he couldn't hold back. He fouled this one weakly down the first base line. One and one.

Jimmy signaled for a fastball inside and high. He thrust his index finger down harder than I had ever seen him, which was our sign for real smoke. He wanted my hardest pitch.

I gave it all I had, and it tailed in on Cory. He swung and missed, and I was pleasantly surprised to be ahead of him one and two. That would give us the chance to waste a pitch or two, hoping to get him to go after something unhittable.

Meanwhile, Cory kept chirping at Jimmy about Star Diamond, and I knew Jimmy would rather have me throw at his head than strike him out. But, hey, Jimmy and Cory and I were friends. I was closer to Jimmy, of course, but Cory went with us to Sunday school and church and was as new a Christian as Jimmy. We could get mad at each other and feud a little, but we didn't really want to hurt each other.

I sure wanted to strike him out, though.

I thought Cory might expect a pitch low and away on one and two, and Jimmy must have agreed. He called for one low and in to cross him up. Cory had shortened up on the bat and stepped close to protect the plate. He jumped back at the last instant. Two and two.

Now the pitch low and away? Cory probably thought so. We jammed him again. Same result. I was irritated that I hadn't been closer with the pitch to either get it on the corner or make it tempting enough to make him swing. Now it was three and two, and I would have to get a pitch over the plate somewhere or risk walking him and losing the deal for Jimmy.

Cory dug in deep, hands a couple of inches up on the bat, ready for anything. No matter how confident he looked, I was certain he had no idea whether we'd come inside again or try low and away to get him out. I wondered if we might not want to try something high and right down the middle. That would surprise him, but if it was that hittable, he'd likely adjust in time and smash it.

Jimmy must have been thinking the same thing. He sat without giving a signal for a while. To throw Cory off I shook my head a couple of times, even before Jimmy started his signals. He called for an offspeed pitch on the outside corner. Great call. I didn't dare throw a ball, but to put a pitch in the strike zone at the same speed I'd been throwing would have been suicidal too.

I have to admit I threw a beautiful pitch. It looked like a fastball until it left my hand. Then it was clearly a slow, moving change-up that appeared headed for the heart of the plate about belt high. It had so little on it, though, that as it swept toward the outside corner, it also dropped to below Cory's knees. He was completely fooled. He began his swing too early, had his front foot too far to the left, and wound up lunging for the pitch.

He got the end of his bat on the ball and dribbled it up the first base line to Jack, who fielded it in foul territory.

Jimmy stood and threw down his glove. I kicked at the dirt on the mound. "We had you," Jimmy said.

"Almost," Cory said. "You almost did. Who knows? You still might."

Jimmy called for the same pitch, but with smoke.

I threw it right on the money, and Cory was fooled again. He fought off the pitch with a weak swing and dribbled it right back to the mound. We got him, but he hadn't struck out. I fielded the ball and raised my eyebrows in a silent congratulations. That wasn't enough for Cory.

"Nice pitch and no hit!" he admitted. "But no strikeout. Nobody strikes out the king!"

"Oh, give me a break!" Jimmy said.

"What'd ya say, cowboy? Can I ride your horse, or isn't he tame enough for me? Better get Jack to give him some more sugar, huh? I wouldn't want him to throw me!"

"Knock it off, Cory," I said. "Jimmy called a perfect sequence of pitches there. Made you look sick."

"Yeah, but you didn't strike me out, and that was the deal! I earned the right to make fun of Jimmy and his stupid horse!"

4

The Announcement

The next day Jimmy was late for our usual pre-practice meeting in the shed behind our barn. Ryan wondered aloud if maybe Jimmy was mad about Cory teasing him so much.

"Oh, I didn't tease him that much. Anyway, he's got it coming to him. That stupid make-believe horse of his!"

"You were a little rough on him, Cor'," Bugsy said.

"Hey, man, I've heard you do the same!"

"Yeah," Bugsy said, "but I know when to quit. You don't."

Cory shook his head.

"He's right," I said. Cory glared at me. "You're supposed to be his friend."

"I am his friend. Only friends will tell you the truth. If I was goin' crazy actin' like a four-year-old, I'd want you guys to tell me."

"Are you serious?" Ryan asked.

"Course!"

"You mean it?"

"Yes!"

"Well then, as a friend I'm gonna tell ya."

"Tell me what?"

"That you're actin' like a jerk, two maybe three years younger than you are. You sound like a spoiled brat, braggin' about your hitting and being an obnoxious know-it-all about Jimmy and his horse."

Cory was so stunned he didn't know what to say. Nobody, especially little Ryan, had ever spoken to him that way before.

Ryan continued. "I don't know why Jimmy still pretends he's got a horse. It's just fun for him. He must want one so bad that this is the best he can do. I agree it sounds a little childish, but why don't you just tell him that, as a friend, and quit making fun of him all the time?"

"He can take it," Cory said, his face as red as his hair now. "He's a big boy."

"Yeah? So where is he?"

"Who knows? I'm not his babysitter!"

I could tell from the look on his face that Cory was surprised that no one agreed with him and that he realized he was wrong. He just wasn't ready to admit it. "All right, guys," I said, "everybody over to the Fergusons' and get started. Bugs, you pitch. Jack, you catch."

"Oh, boy," Jack said. "Do I get to wear the equipment and everything?"

"Yeah, but Jimmy has his own. Take the team stuff from the box outside the shed here. Cory, hang back with me."

"What?"

"Wait till the other guys are gone."

"Oh, brother! Am I in for a sermon?"

I didn't answer. Cory shook his head in disgust. He sure had a lot of growing up to do. But then, so did I.

"Let's walk to the Fergusons'. We can talk on the way."

"No way, man! That's more'n ten minutes!"

"You're in shape."

"I know, but I don't wanna have to walk all the way back here for my bike!"

"Oh, poor baby! Just come on."

"No way!"

"Cory."

"Oh, now you're gonna pull that president-of-the-sports-club routine on me and make me do what you say. I'm already on parole or probation or whatever you call it for the way I stuck up for Nate before he got kicked out."

I didn't say anything. If I let him keep talking he would decide out loud whether he wanted to be in or out. Nathan had been trouble since the first day, and eventually we voted to kick him out. We gave him all kinds of chances to improve, but it was no use.

We never did tell him of the vote, because he quit on his own. That made it easier. But when Cory had stuck up for him and insisted we were all wrong, we put Cory on probation. For a month he had to be careful not to do anything that would get him kicked out. I had never reminded him of it, not even when he was bugging Jimmy or being hostile. He had brought up the subject himself.

I knew he would settle down. He sure didn't want to get kicked out. Not when he was hitting almost .500 and had made a lot of new friends. He had become a Christian, and though he still had a lot of rough edges, he was coming along.

I started walking toward the ball field, and Cory came with me. "Man, I really don't need this," he said.

"I think you do."

"Well, who do you think you are, some pastor or something?"

I shook my head and didn't say anything.

"Well, come on, O'Neil. Out with it. I'll take it like a man. I promise."

"It doesn't sound like it."

"Well, man, O'Neil! It's just that sometimes you come off like you think you're better than everybody."

"I don't think I'm better than anybody."

"Then why are you walkin' me to baseball practice like a bad little boy, gettin' ready to scold me for acting up or whatever?"

"It's part of my job, my responsibility as president of the club."

"Well, it's not like you're perfect or anything."

"I know. I've done things wrong too, and I've apologized."

"Is that what you want me to do? Because if it is, I'm not gonna do it."

"Then forget I'm in charge of the club. Just listen to me as a friend who's a Christian, just like you."

"Oh, but you're not a Christian just like me, Dallas. You're so much better. You know better, you know more, you're a better person. You're so good you can tell me what's wrong with my life and how I should live it."

I gave up. He had won. I didn't want or need a reputation like that, and if he didn't want my help, he sure wasn't going to get it. I fell silent and just trudged along with him.

Finally he spoke. "Oh, so now you're not gonna say anything? I hurt your feelings?"

"Sort of."

"Oh, good. Then I can give your speech for you. You'd probably say, 'Cory, you're a Christian. Christians don't make fun of their friends, even if they are acting weird. Take it easy on Jimmy, understand that he really wants a horse, and pray for him. Don't be mean to him.' "

I shrugged.

"How'd I do?" he asked, smiling.

"I couldn't have said it better myself."

"How does it feel to be so predictable?"

"Not so good. I wonder why I waste my breath."

"Me too. Why don't you put a lid on it and let me live the way I want?"

"Well, since you know how you should treat Jimmy, why don't you treat him that way?"

36

Cory shook his head in disgust. "Man, O'Neil, you just don't get it, do you? I'm not gonna let you live my life for me or tell me how to live it. OK? You got that? Kick me out of the sports club if you want, but I gotta be my own person."

"I don't understand you, Cory," I said. "You know what's right, and you don't want to do it."

"Sounds like you're startin' to understand me, O'Neil."

When we got to the field, Jimmy still wasn't there. Jack looked bigger than ever in the tiny chest protector and shin guards, but he was doing a good job catching. Toby and Ryan had already hit, Ryan smacking a couple in the creek, as usual.

"You can take over pitchin'," Bugsy said. "I'm ready to hit."

"Hear anything from Jimmy?" I asked, taking the ball.

"Nope. No sign of him."

"Maybe he had to feed his horse," Cory said.

Nobody laughed.

Bugsy was hitting when Jimmy showed up on his bike. No reins, no saddle bags, no name on the fender. He let the bike fall by the backstop.

I wondered what in the world was going on, but I knew I wouldn't have to ask.

"Hey, cowboy!" Cory said. "Your horse die?"

"My horse is more alive than it's ever been. Dallas, can I make an announcement?"

"Sure. C'mon in, guys, and take a break."

We sat around the mound.

"After practice," Jimmy said, "after you guys have dumped off your equipment in Dallas's shed, I want you to come over to my place to see my new horse."

I knew he was telling the truth from the way he looked and from what his father had told me. No one else believed him, and I mean no one.

"Oh, come on, Calabresi," Cory snapped. "You've gone haywire now!"

"I can't come," Jack said suddenly. "My dad's pickin' me up at Dallas's shed after I leave my stuff there."

"You can see it next week," Jimmy said.

"Tell us about it, Jim," I said.

"Oh, Dallas," Bugsy said, "you don't believe him, do you?"

"I do."

"It's true," Jimmy said.

"So, tell us," I said.

"Well, he's a golden palomino — "

With that, Cory jumped to his feet with a groan and grabbed a baseball. "I've heard enough of this baloney," he said. "Let's play some ball."

"Sit down, Cory," I said.

He ignored me. "You know how I know he's lying?" Cory said.

"I'm *not* lying! His name's Star Diamond and—"

"Oh, really, Calabresi! What a surprise! If you really got the horse of your dreams, no baseball practice would tear you away from him. Why didn't you ride him over here?"

"Because my dad wouldn't let me. I have to learn to ride him better first."

Cory waved at him with scorn. "I'm not gonna get suckered into comin' over to your place just to see some broomstick with reins, or whatever you're using for a horse now that your bike horse died."

"No," Jimmy said, "listen. My dad made this big sale and got enough money to help me buy Star Diamond. It's like I've known this horse all my life, but I'd never seen him before. He was the one I was dreaming about and pretending to have. This is the happiest day of my life, and nothing you can say or do could spoil it."

"So, how could you pull away from this dream horse for baseball practice?"

"The only thing more fun than having him and getting to know him is telling you guys about him and inviting you over to meet him."

"Oh, sure. How many believe Jimmy has a real, live horse, one that we can see and touch and smell?"

I raised my hand. So did Jack. All the others just sat there.

"Well," Jimmy said, "you'll see."

"I won't," Cory said. "Huh-uh, not me."

"Oh, come on, Cory," I said. "What's the harm in checking it out?"

"And get laughed at by Jimmy because he fooled us? No."

"We'll shut down practice a little early, and anybody who wants to go can go. Jimmy, you want to hit?"

"Yeah, but I might not do too well, as excited as I am."

Cory shook his head in wonder. "Man, O'Neil, you are so gullible I can't believe it."

5

The Chore

As soon as practice was over, we all went back to the shed at my place and dropped off bats, balls, gloves, and shoes. Mrs. Ferguson, the widow who let us put a ball field on her property, wouldn't allow us to install a big wood box with a padlock so we could leave our stuff there. Something about insurance or something. She didn't want to take responsibility if anything happened to our equipment.

That was all right. It gave us a reason to come to my shed before and after practice, and that allowed us to work together like the true club we were. We cared for all our business when we were picking up our equipment, and we made any announcements and arrangements for the future when we were dropping it off.

On the way back to the shed Cory and I caught rides with a couple of the other guys. We would never have ridden double in the city with traffic all around, but out in the country we could rumble along, two on a bike, and not see so much as a pickup truck for miles.

Back at the shed I announced the time and place of our next game. We had finally got permission to play a team from the Park City Little League across the highway. They would be in uniform, just like us, and we would have an umpire. The best thing about it was that there would be lots of fans. That would be something new for us. Park City has nice stands for spectators, and there would be another game going at the other diamond, so lots of people would watch us just out of curiosity.

"This will be the nicest field we've ever played on," I told the guys. "Grass infield, dirt base paths, metal fences, real dugouts, a press box, a public address announcer, everything."

Even Cory was impressed. "Wow," he said, "this is going to be great. I hope I didn't do or say anything today that will keep me from starting and leading off."

"If I was coaching this team," Toby said, "you'd be history."

"You?" Bugsy said. "You've been as hard on Jimmy as anybody."

"Guys," Jimmy said, silencing them with a wave, "it's all right. None of that bothers me anymore. I've got my horse, and I want you all to meet him."

"Oh, I get it," Cory said, "we're all going to traipse over to Jimmy's and pretend he has a horse. What fun! Count me out!"

"All right," I said. "Anybody who wants to go to Jimmy's to see Star Diamond can go right after we're through here. Right, Jim?"

"Right. I'm going to be feeding him, and then I'm going to be riding him for a while, just so we can get used to each other. I'd like to be able to ride him to practice within a day or two and then to the Park City game."

"And you can't do that until you and the horse get to know each other?" Cory pestered.

Jimmy was so excited about his horse that he would not get rattled. "I just want to be sure he's comfortable with me and that I know how to handle him when I'm away from home. Horses are big and can be dangerous, you know."

"Yeah," Cory said. "Especially real ones."

"Mine's real enough," Jimmy said. "He weighs twelve hundred pounds."

A couple of the guys whistled. I could tell most of them still didn't believe Jimmy had a horse. Only Ryan, Toby, Bugsy, and I agreed to go with Jimmy.

I announced the practice schedule for the next two days and the line-up for the Park City game three days later. We would practice all day the next day and for two hours the next. Then we'd be ready for the game. I would pitch. Jimmy would catch. Jack would play first, Cory second, Toby third, Bugsy short, Ryan left, speedy Brent center, and Andy right.

"The batting order will be Cory, Bugsy, me, Toby, Jack, Ryan, Brent, Jimmy, and Andy."

"That's a relief," Cory said.

"If you want to know the truth, Cory," I said. "You're on thin ice."

"Don't worry about me," he said, reddening and making me wish I hadn't said that in front of all the guys (even though he had embarrassed Jimmy in front of everyone). "I want to play."

We dumped our stuff in a corner of the shed, and most of the guys headed home. Ryan, Toby, Bugsy, and I followed Jimmy to his place. If I had any doubts before, they disappeared when I noticed that Jimmy had not only taken all the horse stuff off his bike, he didn't even pretend to ride his bike like a horse. That was something new.

When we got to his house, however, the doubts in everybody's minds grew again. There was no horse in the corral.

Now it was big Toby's turn to take on Jimmy. "What is this?" he demanded. "You think we're as crazy as you are? You gonna pretend there's a horse here?"

"Here!" Jimmy said. "Look at his tracks, right here in the corral."

We edged in and saw hundreds of hoof prints.

"I don't know how you did that," Ryan said, "but until I see that twelve- hundred-pound golden palomino, I'm not believing he's real."

Bugsy said, "Let's get out of here. Man, Jimmy, I almost believed you."

"Wait!" Jimmy said, "Wait a minute! Let me ask my mom where he is. She'll know."

"Well, hurry up. We gotta get goin'."

Jimmy ran to the house. "Mom, Mom! Where's Star Diamond?"

"Your dad took him to the vet. Should be home in an hour or so."

"Mrs. Calabresi," Bugsy said, "is it true—about the horse, I mean?"

"It most certainly is. Jimmy got the horse he always wanted, not a thoroughbred, but with enough Arabian palomino in him that he's golden with a very light tail and mane. It's as if he were born to be Jimmy's horse."

"Why'd he have to go to the vet?" Jimmy asked.

"I'm not sure," his mother said. "Nothing's wrong. It's just that your father got a call at work today and was told that the horse had to have some kind of shots or tests or something as soon as possible after he's settled in his new home."

"You know what?" Toby said, smiling so none of us could tell if he was kidding or not. "I'm still not sure I believe this. You guys remember the time we had that costume party and Mrs. Calabresi came with Mrs. O'Neil and made everybody think, for the whole night, that she was Mr. O'Neil. It was fantastic."

"Oh, that's just because I'm tall and kept my mouth shut all night. It was Dallas's mom who convinced everyone I was her husband. I was dressed like the King of Siam."

"Yeah, but you're a pretty good fooler anyway," Toby said, "and you always like to go along with a good practical joke. I gotta tell ya, I'm not buying this yet. I think we're all in for a good laugh."

"No, I'm telling you the truth on this one, Toby. Trust me."

But there was just enough of a twinkle in her eye, and a smile on Jimmy's face, that I began to have new doubts myself. Jimmy and his mother fell silent, and the rest of us looked at each other.

Ryan shook his head, smiling. "I don't believe this," he said. "Cory was right! We've been had!"

"No, you haven't," Jimmy said. "You'll see!"

"I gotta go," Bugsy said. "How 'bout the rest of you suckers?"

We turned and started out, but Mrs. Calabresi had another idea. "Jimmy, I just remembered something your father said before he left. It's something that will convince your friends you have a horse. He said you've got a chore to do before dinner."

"A chore?"

"Yes, the one you had to agree to before Dad agreed to buy you the horse. I mean, you've got lots of chores and expenses related to that horse, but this is the important one, the one you have to do every morning before breakfast, or you don't eat, remember?"

"I remember. Where's the shovel?"

"Dad left it just inside the stable."

"C'mon, guys!"

We followed Jimmy through the corral to the far end where the stable door was closed and latched. Jimmy slid the wood piece to the side and opened the door.

"Whew! Phew!"

"That's all the convincing I need!" Bugsy said. "I'm not goin' in there!"

"I have to muck out the stall," Jimmy said. "That's the chore I had to agree to do myself everyday."

"Muck out?" Ryan said. "What's that?"

"Shovel out the stall," Jimmy explained.

"Why do you have to shovel it out everyday? Can't you just shovel it out once and for all? I mean, how much dirt can a horse track in in a day?"

"It's not dirt, Ryan," Bugsy said. "Do we have to spell it out for you?"

"No," Ryan said, a grin playing at the corners of his mouth. "I can smell it out for myself. See ya, Jimmy."

Jimmy headed into the stall with his shovel while the rest of us moved toward our bikes.

"All of a sudden I believe Mrs. Calabresi," Toby said.

"Me too, me too," the rest of us chimed in.

"Whew," Bugsy said. "I'm not sure havin' a horse would be worth that."

"They say you get used to the smell after a while," I said.

"Yeah, after about a year."

We laughed as we rode away, shouting good-byes to Jimmy. Ryan and Bugsy and Toby rode north toward Toboggan Road. I peeled off at the corner and headed for Baker Street.

As I neared our place, I saw a pickup truck pulling a horse wagon, heading my way. It could only be Jimmy's dad. No one else around had a horse, even though we all lived in places that had enough room and were zoned for a horse per acre. I waited at the side of the road and waved as he came fully into view.

As I was hoping he'd do, Mr. Calabresi slowly pulled off on the other side of the road and waved me over. He stepped out of the truck. "Wanna see Star Diamond?" he said.

"Sure!"

"You see why this was such an expensive proposition? I had the pickup, but I had to buy a used horse trailer. Not cheap."

"I'll bet."

He took me to the trailer where a long, horizontal window revealed only the horse's side. "C'mon around back," he said.

When he opened the door, the horse grew skittish and stepped back and forth, as if he thought he was getting out.

"Whoa, not yet, boy," Mr. Calabresi said, smacking him on the rear. "Course you can't see much from this angle, but he's a beauty, isn't he?"

"He sure is. I know why Jimmy's excited." I told him how no one had believed Jimmy or his mother until she came up with a way to convince us.

He thought that was hilarious.

"You want to ride him? Follow me home."

"I have to be home in five minutes, but thanks anyway. Maybe I'll get a chance tomorrow."

"Maybe. But I think Jimmy's planning to ride him yet tonight. Maybe he'll bring him by."

"That'd be great."

"You ride, don't you, Dallas?"

"Yes, sir. I had a horse."

"That's right! Lightning. Beautiful white stallion."

I could hardly speak. I almost cried every time I thought of that horse. That's why, even though I was happy for Jimmy, I had no interest in riding his gorgeous new palomino.

6

Star Diamond

The horse was magnificent. I couldn't argue that. I was jealous. I couldn't argue that either. I didn't dwell on it. It just hurt. I had had a beautiful horse and now didn't have one. Jimmy had always dreamed of having one and now did. He was enough of a friend that I couldn't resent him for his good fortune. I guess I felt like my uncle felt when he visited us just after my baby sister Jennifer was born. My uncle and his wife had lost a baby a few weeks before, so even though he would put his hand on Jenny's tummy and smile at her, he would not hold her. Now I understood why.

I'm sure Jimmy's dad told him of having shown me Star Diamond on the way home, and he probably even said that he had half promised that I could ride the horse that night if Jimmy rode by. That's why I was surprised when I saw Jimmy and Star Diamond trotting by while I was doing my chores.

The horse was not galloping but not cantering either. He was just trotting along with Jimmy firmly in the saddle, eyes straight ahead, a look of deep concentration on his face. He rode past our house, on the other side of Baker Street, and a few minutes later he came back the same way on the same side. He must have passed our place six or eight times, always at the same speed, always with Jimmy holding on tight, staring, concentrating. I remembered that Jimmy had never ridden a horse before, except for those ponies that walk in a circle with a trainer next to them. He was probably scared to death.

The next morning we all showed up at the shed to talk and get our stuff. Jimmy was there with his bike, and he was beaming.

"Did anyone actually see that horse?" Cory demanded. "I told you there was no horse. You guys all got your chops busted."

"I smelled it," Bugsy said.

"Me too," Ryan said. "Unless they shipped in horse manure, they got a horse there all right."

"I believe there's a horse," Toby said, "'cause I can't imagine anyone going to the trouble of mucking out a stall if he didn't really have to. But I didn't see a horse. I can't swear he's got one."

"And even if he does," Cory said, "there's no provin' it's some giant yellow palomino. Probably an old gray nag. Anyway, if this horse you've always wanted landed in your pretend corral, how come you didn't ride it today?"

Jimmy sighed and shook his head. "I'm not ready to bring him out and leave him tied to the backstop yet. But I will."

"Oh, sure, Jimmy. Sure."

I had to speak up. "I saw the horse," I said. "It's huge, and it's golden, and it has a white mane, or at least a lighter colored mane, maybe cream, and the same for its tail. It's one beautiful animal. I can't wait till you guys see it."

"Oh," Cory said, "and I'm so sure we're supposed to believe you. Everybody knows you guys are best friends and are in this thing together. What are you tryin' to prove?"

"Cory," I said, "if we were pulling some kind of a trick on you, don't you think we could come up with something better than pretending Jimmy got his horse? I mean, what would be the point of that?"

"I don't know. Maybe at the end of it all you just laugh at us and tell us you got us."

"Oh, that'd be great fun," I said. "I think we could do better than that."

Not even Toby was totally convinced. "Where'd you see this horse, Dallas?"

"Jimmy's dad was driving it home from the vet, and I saw him on the road. He showed me. Then Jimmy came riding past my house a half dozen times or so."

"Yeah," Jimmy said, "sorry I didn't stop, but I didn't really know how. I didn't even dare look up to see if you saw us, and I'm glad you didn't yell. You might have spooked Star Diamond."

"I know better than that, " I said. "I wondered why you didn't come over."

Jimmy looked embarrassed. "I don't really know how to do much besides stop him and turn him around. I wasn't sure I could get him across the road, and I sure didn't want to scare him and have him take off on me."

"Where'd you come up with the name for that horse, anyway?" Cory asked. "It sure is stupid."

"Cory," I said. "You're cruising."

"Sorry. I'm really wonderin' though."

Bugsy said, "I figured that out a long time ago. It's backward for Diamond Star, and that's what Jimmy thinks he is."

Jimmy laughed.

Cory said, "Oh, brother! Is that true?"

"Not even close," Jimmy said. "There's nothing really exciting about it. Matter of fact, I saw the name Diamond Star on a piano in Dallas's church basement. I always liked those words, especially together, and so I switched 'em around and named my horse that."

"Your play horse."

"For a while he was a play horse, but I knew he was alive somewhere. And now I've got him."

"I'll believe that when I see it."

"You will."

That day, since we were planning on practicing pretty much all day except for a break at lunch time, my plan was to let everybody get lots of batting practice.

"All day BP!" Cory said. "All right! We gonna hit in the batting order?"

"Yup," I said, not thinking. We always took batting practice in the batting order, but lately Andy had been asking if we couldn't reverse it occasionally so he didn't always have to wait till last to hit. I promised him we would, but I forgot until after I had said we would hit in order. I saw the stricken look on his face and should have either changed my decision or said something to Andy about forgetting.

Andy needed as much BP as anybody. That's why he hit last and played right field. On the other hand, we didn't count on him for much offense, so what did it hurt if he waited to get in his swings? The only problem was, he wasn't convinced he was the ninth best hitter on the team. He told me once he thought he should be leading off. He also thought he could play catcher better than Jimmy. I tried him out a few times, but he could neither catch nor throw as well as Jimmy. I left him where he was. He really didn't complain that much. I told him everybody was important to the team and that somebody had to bat ninth, and somebody had to play right.

"But I gotta do both?"

"For now, yes."

"At least let us take BP in reverse order once in a while."

I promised I would, but so far I hadn't. Maybe tomorrow.

I pitched to Cory and Bugsy, then Bugsy pitched to me while Toby covered both third and short. That way, we stayed in our positions as much as possible and hit in game situations. I would call out how many were out and what runners were on which bases, then we would play it straight.

The pitching was easy, to save our arms for the games, but we played every hit like it as the real thing. On the last swing, the batter had to run, and there were slides, pick offs, steals, rundowns, you name it. I always encouraged the guys to try to stretch singles into doubles and doubles into triples. We were unusually fast in the first third and last third of our lineup, and unusually slow in the middle. Toby, Jack, and Jimmy were nowhere as fast as the other guys on the team, though Jack was surprisingly fast for his size.

Still, I encouraged all that extra base taking, because I wanted the fielders and basemen to work on their throws and tags. "Don't worry if you're out! This is for the defense!"

Especially I wanted the fast guys to see how often they would be successful in stretching a hit. It seemed that, more often than not, forcing a kid our age to make a throw or a tag resulted in an error and success for the offense.

Though I was not pitching my best, not trying to strike anybody out, I did try to move the ball around a lot and keep it low. I also changed speeds from three-quarter to very slow. It was good for the guys, I thought.

Cory never even swung and missed. He had somehow developed that ability to get the bat on the ball so that it took a very good fastball or a really moving curve to get him to miss it. He didn't even hit many fouls. He was constantly getting the ball in play. I just wished his attitude was at the same level as his skills.

He was pretty good at second base too. When Bugsy ran out his last hit, he drove the ball on one hop to Brent in left.

"Come up firing!" I shouted. "Cory, you're covering second!"

"I know, I know!" Cory yelled, clearly irritated. "I always cover on hits to left."

He drifted over to the bag while Toby went out to take the relay. Bugsy raced toward second, dirt flying up behind him. Brent pegged the ball right at Toby's head like he was supposed to, and at the last instant Cory shouted, "Let it go!" Rather than cutting it off, Toby ducked, letting the ball sail right to Cory's glove.

53

Bugsy dove into a long, headfirst slide. Cory took the throw about shoulder high and swept it down in front of the bag. Bugsy slid right into it.

"Nice play, boys!" I said.

Bugsy jumped up kicking the dirt. "It sure was," he said. "I wasn't stretching that just for practice. I was testing Brent's arm, and I thought it had been hit slow enough so I could get away with it. I hope Park City tries something that stupid."

"You mean stretching a hit or trying to throw you out?"

"Either one. Which team are we playing over there, anyway?"

"Beattie's Drug Store."

"Seriously? Last year's city champs? The one with the big, hard throwing right-hander?"

I nodded. "And I happen to know he's pitching against us." There were moans and groans all around. "C'mon!" I said. "You guys like fast pitching. That's all he's got. The ball never moves, never changes speeds. He blows it by us for three innings or so, then he tires a little, and we get our timing down. Then he's history."

"Oh, no," Bugsy said, "does that mean what I think it means?"

"Depends," I said. "What do you think it means?"

"That we have to face Matt and Kyle in batting practice tomorrow?"

"Exactly."

More moaning and groaning. "Dallas, those guys throw harder than you do, but they have no control. We're gonna be bailin' out on every pitch, scared for our heads and our lives."

"That's the whole point," I said. "You'll get used to that speed, and when the big guy—Frank Tibbitts—throws it in there with control, it'll look easy."

"Sure, if any of us survive Matt and Kyle." Toby smiled.

"C'mon, Dallas!" Andy called from right field. "I wouldn't mind getting in a few swings today myself."

I couldn't blame Andy. Because I ended practice early the day before so we could see Jimmy's horse, he had missed getting his hitting time. I was letting everybody hit for between ten and twenty minutes. We needed the work. The chance to face a team like Beattie's and a pitcher like Tibbitts was something we couldn't pass up.

7

The Grand Slam

We took a long lunch break that day, longer than usual by far. Bugsy got the idea for everybody to dump their equipment at my shed, ride home and pack themselves lunches, and meet back at the creek that ran past left and center fields. At first I fought the idea. "We wouldn't want to leave any garbage on the Ferguson property."

"We won't, Dallas. Everybody can just put all the trash back in their lunch sacks and toss them in the dump on their way home. And hey, everybody, bring your swimming suits. It's getting hot."

That was sure true. It would be 100 degrees by noon. I just hoped we had enough time for all the batting practice we wanted to do that day. There was only one more day before we faced Beattie's at the Park City field. We couldn't have an all-day practice that day, or we'd be too tired for the game.

The lunch and the swim worked out great, but it did take a long time. We waited almost an hour between the time we quit eating and when we jumped into the creek, and by the time we did, we were burning up. The guys had worn their swimsuits under their jeans or shorts, and we sat in the sun waiting for our food to digest, seeing how hot and red we could get with our shirts off.

That creek felt like ice at first, but it was just what we needed. We knew better than to swim the day before a game, because swimming was exhausting. We played tag, tried to see how long we could stay under water, saw who could drop into the water from the highest branch on the old oak tree, and raced each other to the other side.

We toweled off and gathered up our suits and garbage at about three o'clock, and if anything the temperature was even higher. That was great for baseball practice. Your arm felt loose, you sweated through all your clothes. You really got in shape. I knew it was good for my arm if I didn't overdo it.

After Ryan hit, Brent and Jimmy came in to take their swings.

"Hey," Brent said, "aren't you guys getting tired of this? Let's split up and have a game. I'll skip batting practice if I can be on the team that's up first."

I had to admit he was right. Batting practice all day was a drag. We were all competitive. The guys mostly agreed, though Andy complained about missing his BP again.

"You'll get lots of times up in a game," Jimmy told him.

Andy made a face, and we all lined up to choose sides.

"Who's choosing?" Brent asked.

"It was your idea," I said. "Why don't you choose the visiting team, and, uh, Jimmy, you pick the home team."

Brent chose me first. Jimmy picked Toby. Brent took Cory. Jimmy took Bugsy. Brent picked Jack. Jimmy chose Ryan. That left Andy to be on Brent's team. We had one more player than they did, but they didn't mind because it was Andy. "I sure wish Matt or Kyle were here," Brent said.

We decided to bat in the order we were picked, and the only other rule was that you had to play something other than your usual position.

With just four on one team and five on the other, we wouldn't have catchers. It would be pitcher's hands rather than throwing to first for the out, and there would be two outfielders and two infielders on our team, one infielder and two outfielders on their team. I didn't see how we could have any more fun than this, unless it was in a real game with full teams on both sides. But that was two days away.

Jimmy pitched with Ryan at short and Bugsy and Toby in the outfield. For us, Brent would pitch with Cory and me in the outfield, Andy at second, and Jack at short. Seeing that big guy at short would be an experience.

It was getting hotter by the minute. I didn't know if we could hold out for the whole afternoon or not. We all had hats on and were sweating like crazy. Every time you ran to first or ran after a ball you were winded. It was probably good for us, but we were dragging.

Brent led off with a line drive right back to Jimmy. One out.

I was so eager to hit off Jimmy's nice, straight, fast pitches that I lunged after the first pitch and hit a sharp grounder down the third base line. Ryan dove to snag it, and while still on the ground flipped it to Jimmy for the out. Usually in a pickup game like this each team scores at least four or five runs an inning. We were suddenly faced with two out and nobody on. With Brent pitching for us, we were going to need runs.

Cory was up, and he was taunting Jimmy like everything. "You gonna throw a meadow muffin here, or haven't you already mucked out Star Diamond's stall today?"

Jimmy threw the first pitch right at Cory and hit him in the shoulder. I could see it coming.

Cory jumped to his feet and charged the mound, but I intercepted him. "Jimmy, was that on purpose?" I asked.

"No! He was crowdin' the plate, but I didn't mean to hit him."

"Then apologize."

"Sorry."

"You don't sound like it," Cory said.

"Well, I'm not sayin' it again, crybaby, so take it or leave it."

"Boy," I whispered, "you two are sure being good examples here."

Both looked away, and Cory took first.

Jack came to the plate, swinging the bat like it was a toothpick. Jimmy kept the ball away from him, but with two strikes Jack lifted a high fly between Bugsy and Toby. Toby was closest, but he was just too slow. He grabbed the ball and fired to the plate, holding Cory at third while Jack wound up on second.

Jimmy kicked the dirt. "I really thought we were gonna hold these guys scoreless this inning," he said.

"We still can," Bugsy called in from the outfield. "Walk Andy to load the bases, and we'll put three guys in the infield. Make Brent hit a grounder, and we've got a force at any base."

"All right," Jimmy yelled, "we're walkin' Andy intentionally."

"Go to first," I told him.

Andy threw his bat against the backstop and walked to first. Bugsy and Toby came in from the outfield to give Jimmy's team three infielders and no outfielders. It backfired on them.

Brent hit a texas league dinker into short left and made it to second with the other three scoring. Cory and I hit back-to-back homers before Toby flied out deep to left. We led 5-0, and the mid-afternoon sun was baking us.

Jimmy's team then had one of those half innings that make you wish you'd set a scoring limit. Sometimes we do that. We don't allow a team more than a four run lead. So if one team is down 4-0, the most they can score the next half inning is eight. Well, we didn't set that rule in advance, and I think Jimmy's team was as sorry about it as we were, because there were only four of them, and they had to do all the running.

They got hits, and we made errors, and they had nine runs before we got the first out. Then they scored six more before we finally got another out. With the bases loaded, two out, them leading 15-0, Jimmy hit the longest home-run in the short history of our ball field. Brent had thrown him a chest-high fastball, well out over the plate.

I was playing deep left center field and saw Jimmy turn on the pitch. He got all of it. It went straight up and way out over my head. I didn't even turn to run. I had set up close enough to the creek that I could get to the edge before the ball, but there was no sense turning and running after this one. It was long gone. I just stood and watched it. It completely cleared the creek, and everybody but Andy came out to see where it landed—including Jimmy.

We all ran to the narrowest point in the creek, hopped over, and raced to the spot where the ball had stopped rolling.

"I wouldn't mind measuring this one," Jimmy said, grinning. "Let me mark it with a stick so I can bring back a tape measure later." He searched for a stick to put in the ground near the ball, but Andy complained.

"C'mon, let's get on with it! One more out and I lead off the next inning."

"Oh, no!" Bugsy said. "We're not playin' anymore, are we, Dallas? It's too hot, and we're dead."

"Oh, that's easy for you to say," Cory said. "You're the ones with the fourteen-run lead. That was a nice hit, Jimmy, but you're still lyin' about your horse."

Jimmy ignored him and stuck his stick in the ground.

"I think they're right, Cory," I said. "That's enough for today. Jimmy, why don't you go home and get your tape measure? This must have been a three-hundred footer."

Cory and Andy shook their heads and trudged back across the creek, while most of the other guys gratefully agreed with me and sat under a tree, waiting to see what the measurement would be.

"What a day!" Brent said, lying on his back with his hands behind his head. "I could sleep right here."

A few of the others went back across and sat around the backstop with Cory and Andy. Jimmy rode his bike toward my place to dump off his equipment. He said he would be right back with the tape measure.

From across the creek came a challenge from Cory. "Why don't you come back on your horse, Babe Ruth? If you really have one!"

"Maybe I just will!" Jimmy called over his shoulder.

About twenty minutes later Jimmy did come back on Star Diamond, and the Baker Street Sports Clubbers who were still there gathered around to admire him. Unfortunately, Cory was one of those who had already left.

Jimmy tethered the big horse to a tree, then jogged back to the diamond where he began measuring from home plate to the edge of the creek. It was 253 feet. He held onto one end of the tape and threw the rest across the creek to me. I measured the creek at that point, which was 49 feet, then to the spot where I saw the ball hit the first time. That was another 11 feet. It rolled another 40 feet. We figured Jimmy had hit that grand slam 313 feet in the air and that from home to the spot where it stopped was 353 feet. We knew we'd be talking about that one for years.

Jack was fascinated by Star Diamond. The stallion nuzzled him when he approached, and Jack's eyes grew huge. "I didn't know whether you really had a horse or not, Jimmy," Jack said. "But I'm sure glad you do. Can I ride him?"

"Sorry, Jack. I can't let anyone ride him until I get to know him better. He has to be able to obey my commands, and anyway, my dad only wants other people riding him at our place when he's around."

Jack nodded. "He's sure a beauty." It seemed all the guys there said the same thing. I only wished Cory had hung around to be finally convinced. Matt and Kyle would be joining us for practice the next day, and they would believe Jimmy. It was fun to watch him get more and more comfortable with the horse, guiding it slowly along the creek bank and through the shallow water.

"Practice tomorrow morning, guys," I said. "Let's get in a couple of hours before it gets too hot. Then relax the rest of the day so we'll be ready to face Beattie's."

"Can I bring my horse to practice, Dal?" Jimmy asked.

"Sure, as long as you tie him behind the backstop where he won't get hit with the ball."

Everybody would be there, so everybody would finally know the truth.

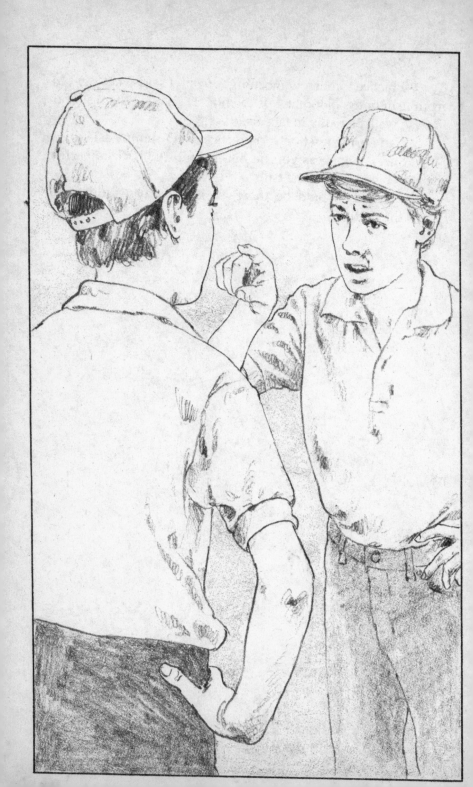

8

The Challenge

Before practice the next day everybody except Cory and Jimmy showed up at our shed. I figured Jimmy might have had some problem with his horse, but I had no idea where Cory might be.

"If Jimmy doesn't show up," I told Matt, "I'd like you to catch today. Kyle, if Cory isn't at practice, I'll need you to lead off and play second."

"Oh, couldn't I?" Andy said.

"No, I want to keep everything pretty much the way it will be against Beattie's tomorrow. If Jimmy and Cory have good excuses, they'll be playing in their regular spots in the field and in the batting order, so these are just temporary substitutions. If Jimmy shows up, Matt, I'll want you to pitch today, and if Cory shows up, Kyle, I'll want you to pitch. If they both come, you guys will both pitch batting practice."

Matt and Kyle both felt good about the situation. They would get lots of practice either way. Andy didn't look too happy, but somebody had to bat ninth and play right. I thought he should be happy to be in the starting lineup. I know Matt or Kyle would have been happy, because they'd told me often enough.

I reminded everybody of the line-up for the next evening and told them we would practice only till noon. "We want to be fresh and sharp—no excuses—against Beattie's."

"All I want is an excuse against Matt and Kyle," Toby said. "I'd rather face Frank Tibbitts."

Everybody laughed. "You'll get your chance soon enough," I said. "We'll see what you say then."

When we got to the field, Cory was there waiting for us, and Jimmy came along soon after—on his bike, not his horse.

"Dad still won't let me bring him to stand around for a couple of hours," he explained. "Sorry I'm late. I was tryin' to talk him into it."

"Where were you, Cory?"

"I was here."

"Why didn't you come to the shed first?"

"Didn't need to. I took my stuff home with me yesterday afternoon."

"Can we take a walk?"

"Oh, brother. What now?"

I motioned for him to follow me. "Kyle! Take second. Matt! Hit infield practice."

Cory fell in step with me, shaking his head.

"You know," I said, "you've always had an attitude problem, but I really thought it would get better once you started coming to church and became a Christian."

"Oh, Dallas, what did I do now?"

"You didn't come to the meeting before practice."

"I told you! I took my stuff home yesterday afternoon."

"That doesn't mean anything. You know we have a meeting every day before practice."

"Well, Jimmy didn't come either, and you didn't get all over his case."

"Jimmy had an excuse, Cory. Maybe it wasn't a very good one, but he also apologized and jumped right into practice. He already has his equipment on, and he's ready to go."

"So am I."

"Cory, you know you're on probation. You want me to call a vote and see what the guys think about whether you should stay in the club?"

"Come on, Dallas! I miss one of your precious little meetings, and you want to run me out of the club. Give me a break! Jimmy gets away with murder and acts like a baby with that crazy horse, or pretend horse, and I get nailed for everything."

I sighed. "Let's get this straight once and for all, Cory. No matter what you think about Jimmy pretending to have a horse for so long, he does have one now. Most of us have seen it, and even if most of us hadn't, I've seen it, and you know I don't lie."

"Oh, no, of course not. You're perfect."

I ignored that remark. "So you don't believe any of us who have seen Star Diamond?"

"I'll believe it when I see it."

"You're making my job real hard, Cory."

"Your job isn't hard, Dallas. Just put me at second base and lead me off. I'll get on two or three times, and you big sticks can drive me in."

"I get it now," I said. "You think you're so good, so important to this team that you can act like a jerk and get away with it."

"I'm not acting like a jerk. You're just afraid of anybody who doesn't obey your every command."

"You think I like or want this job? I'd rather have someone tell me what to do and when to do it. I'd rather have someone else make out the lineup and tell me where to play and when to hit."

"Fine, then tell the guys you'd like me to be president. I'll handle it."

"I wouldn't wish that on my worst enemy." I wished I hadn't said that as soon as it came out of my mouth. It was true, but it sure wasn't kind. "I'm sorry," I added quickly. "I shouldn't have said that."

"Yeah? Well, what's that rule about a vote of confidence?"

"What?"

"You said once that any time anybody wanted to take a vote of confidence for or against the president, he could. If the president didn't get three-fourths of the votes saying he should stay in, the floor would be open for new nominations."

"Yeah, so what?"

"Well, I want a vote of confidence taken about you. Nobody still wants you as president. Everybody's as tired of you as I am."

I was stunned, wondering if he could be right. I'd just been trying to do the job the best way I knew how, but maybe I had become obnoxious. How could I know? Maybe a vote of confidence was what we needed. Cory had gotten me completely off the track of trying to straighten him out.

"All right," I said. "After practice, we'll meet back at the shed for a vote of confidence."

"And a vote for a new president?"

"If I don't get a three-fourths vote of confidence, sure."

"Dallas, by the end of the day, I'll be president of the Baker Street Sports Club, and you can bank on it."

What had I done to deserve this? And what difference had becoming a Christian made in Cory's life? If anything, he was worse than before. As we walked back toward the field, Cory made me promise I would announce the vote right away.

"Like right now," he said.

I called everybody around the mound. "After practice today we're going to have a president's vote of confidence," I said.

"What for?" Jimmy demanded.

"To see if we still want Dallas as president," Cory said.

"What's the point?" Jimmy pressed.

"I just told you," Cory said. "You wouldn't want him to stay president just because he's your best friend, would you?"

"No, but there's been no problem. I don't get it."

"You don't have to get it. I want a vote."

"Can a vote be called by a guy who's on probation? Sounds to me like the problem is with you, not with Dallas."

"Oh, we're gonna make up a new rule now because I'm on probation? Where does it say a guy on probation can't call for a vote of confidence on the president, or run for president himself if he wants? I'm still a full-fledged member of this club, aren't I?"

"Yes, you are," I said miserably. "And anybody can call for a vote."

"Then I'm callin' for one. A secret ballot with the scraps of paper and the can of pencils and everything."

"I say we don't need a vote," Jimmy said.

"I think a vote would be a good idea," Toby said. "What's the harm?"

I was shocked. Toby wanted a vote too?

"Yeah," Bugsy said. "A vote couldn't hurt."

"I vote for Dallas," Jack said.

"We're not voting now, you big dummy!" Cory said, and everybody glared at him. Jack looked hurt.

"OK, all right, I'm sorry," Cory said. "But we're still votin'—right after practice."

Ryan raised his hand. "Dallas," he said, "I can't be here for the game tomorrow. We're going to my aunt and uncle's. I can't get out of it."

"You can still vote this afternoon, can't you?" Cory asked.

"I guess."

I was disappointed that Ryan would not be in the game against Beattie's. From the beginning he had been one of our best hitters, a surprisingly strong power hitter for an average-sized kid. He had dropped to sixth in the batting order only when Toby and Jack began driving the ball so consistently.

"Matt," I said, "I'll want you to play left and bat sixth tomorrow."

"OK!"

"In fact, Ryan, if you wouldn't mind pitching today, Matt can play left during practice and get used to it."

Andy spoke up. "Why don't you put Matt ninth in the order and move the rest of us up?"

"Because I want to keep the order and the lineup as close to normal as possible," I snapped. "That's why."

"But I'm a better hitter than Matt, or he would be starting in right, wouldn't he?"

"Andy, for right now I'm captain, and that means I set the lineup. Why don't you play and let me manage, OK?"

"OK, O'Neil. Grief!"

I felt bad for having lashed out at him, but how much of this junk was a guy supposed to take? "Let's practice!"

Normally during practice the day before a game I'm pitching, I just watch from behind the backstop, shouting encouragement and instructions. This day, though, I really felt out of it. Cory was jogging around to individual players and talking to them, probably trying to raise support for his cause.

He was the first to hit, of course, and when he was finished and Bugsy was stepping in, I heard Cory say, "Of course I'll run for president. That's the whole point."

When it was my turn to hit I was so distracted by Cory's challenge of my leadership that I hardly noticed that Ryan might soon become a good pitcher. He's always had a strong arm, but now he seemed to have excellent control. It was hard to ask for more than that.

My last swing was a double between left and center, and I slid into second under Cory's tag.

"I've already got enough votes to beat you," he said.

I didn't say anything.

By the end of practice, when Andy was hitting, Kyle was on the mound and couldn't find the plate. Andy took six or seven straight pitches over his head or in the dirt, but for some reason, instead of hollering at Kyle to start getting the ball in there, the guys started badgering Andy to start swinging. "C'mon! Some of those are hittable. Let's go! Let's get this over with!"

Before Andy even hit one, the guys started drifting off the field toward their bikes. I had lost my courage to tell them to get back to practice, and, with no fielders, Kyle eventually quit pitching. Once again, Andy didn't get in any decent batting practice.

Within a few minutes everybody was heading for my place and the shed. No one would miss this meeting.

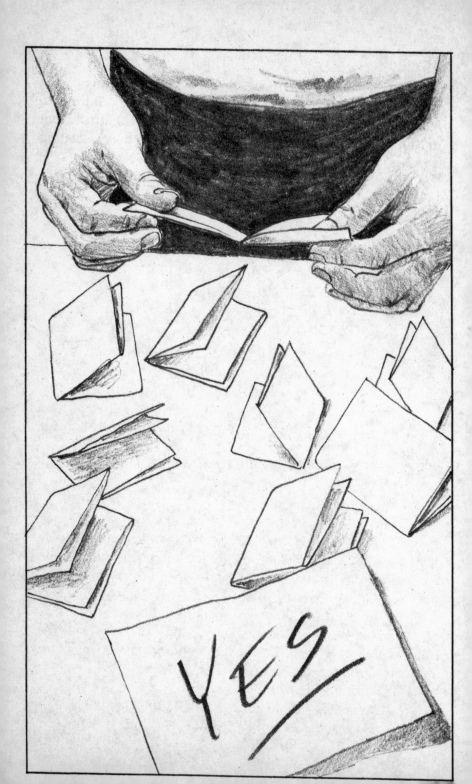

9

The Vote

I was pretty somber when I opened the meeting. All eleven of us were there, and Cory was ready.

"I think the secretary should call the roll," he said.

"Oh, come on, Cory," Jimmy said. "I'm the secretary, and I can see that everybody's here. You want somebody to take minutes, too?"

"We've never done that, but maybe with a new president we would."

"Suit yourself," I said.

"Is the meeting officially open?" he asked.

"Yes," I said, "and in the absence of an agenda I'll open the floor for any old business." I waited a moment. "In the absence of any old business, the floor is open for any new business."

"Point of order," Cory said, making me wish our school wasn't so big on teaching elementary kids all about Roberts Rules of Order. It seemed there was nothing we argued about more than little points of order in every meeting.

"Yes, Cory."

"I still think we should have an official calling of the roll."

"I would entertain a motion," I said.

"I move we waive the calling of the roll," Jimmy said.

"Hey, I disagree with that," Cory said.

"You're out of order, Cory," I said. "If you want to follow the rules, you can't discuss a motion until it has been seconded."

"Second," Ryan said. "Forget calling the roll. We're all here."

"Hey! He's discussing the motion."

"He seconded it, so he can do that."

"Well, can I discuss it now? Can I say why I'll be voting against it?"

"Sure."

"It won't hurt anything to call the roll. We're gonna have a secret ballot here in a while, and this will help us know exactly how many are officially here and all that."

"Any other discussion?"

"I agree with Cory," Toby said. "Let's call the roll."

"We can't call the roll unless this motion is passed. Do you want to vote on the motion?"

"No," Bugsy said. "I want to speak to it too."

"Go ahead."

"I don't think there'd be any more harm in calling the roll than waiving the roll call, so why don't we defeat this motion and call the roll?"

"If you all feel that way," Jimmy said, "I'll withdraw the motion to waive."

"No," Cory said, "I want to see your motion get beat!"

"That's all I needed to hear," Jimmy said. "I withdraw my motion."

"This is getting crazy," I said. "Let's get on with the meeting."

"Then have the secretary call the roll!" Cory said.

"Not unless I get a motion and a second and that motion carries."

"All right, so moved," Cory said.

"Second," Jimmy said.

I couldn't believe it. "Now you're on his side?" I said.

"I just want to get out of here."

"All right, any discussion?"

Everyone, for once, was silent. "All in favor?" All raised their hands, though Jack was the last to raise his. Cory beamed in victory.

"Call the roll, Jimmy," I said.

"Yeah," Cory said, "and start with Star Diamond."

"Not funny, Cory," I said. "Knock it off."

I knew I was not making a good show as a cool-headed president, but part of me didn't care. What if I did lose the vote of confidence and then got voted out of office? I tried to tell myself it wouldn't make any difference, that my life would be easier. Meanwhile, Jimmy called the roll in alphabetical order by first names.

"Andy?"

"Here."

"Brent?"

"Here."

"Bugsy?"

"Here."

"Cory?"

"Am I ever!"

"Dallas?"

"Yo."

"Jack?"

"What?"

"Just say 'Here' if you're here."

"Of course I'm here!"

"Jimmy? Here! Kyle?"

"Here."

"Matt?"

"Here."

"Ryan?"

"Here."

"Toby?"

"Here."

"All present and accounted for, Mr. President," Jimmy said.

Cory laughed. "Don't get too used to that title, Dallas."

I gave him a look of disgust. "Any new business?"

"I move we adjourn," Jimmy said.

I was so proud of Jimmy I could hardly stand it. I knew Cory would never let him get away with that, but it was a stalling technique and if it got a second, we'd have to vote on it before moving on to new business.

"Hey," Cory shouted, "you can't do that! We haven't had new business yet!"

"The motion hasn't been seconded," I said, "so you can't discuss it yet."

"But it's out of order!"

"You're out of order!" I said. "Is there a second to the motion to adjourn?" I waited. "Hearing none, I'll second the motion."

"No!" Cory said. "No way! The chair can't make or second motions, and you can't even vote unless it's to break a tie."

I knew he was right. "The chair apologizes and withdraws the second. Is there a second?"

"Second!"

It was Jack, and Cory flew into a rage. "He doesn't even know what he's doing!"

"I do too!" Jack said. "I want to second something, and I'll second this!"

"You've got to overrule that, Dallas," Jimmy said.

"I won't," I said. "He's a full member of this club just like you are, and he has the same rights."

"Call for the question," Toby said.

"All those in favor of adjourning, please raise your hand."

Jimmy and I raised our hands. So did Jack, who said, "I want to adjourning."

"You can't vote, Dallas!" Cory repeated. "Unless it's to break a tie."

"The chair apologizes. My vote will be ignored. All against the motion, the same sign."

Everyone else raised his hand.

"Motion denied. We will not adjourn. Is there any new business?"

Cory was ready. "I call for a vote of confidence on the president by secret ballot."

"Second," Toby said.

He said it so quickly I wondered if he had been ready too. They must have talked about it in advance. But I couldn't remember ever having had any problems with Toby. Not one.

"Any discussion?"

"Yeah," Cory said, "I wanna know how many votes we need to vote you out."

I asked Jimmy to figure it out.

"I'll need a pencil and paper," he said.

"So will the rest of us," Cory said. "The motion was for secret ballot, remember?"

"Your motion still has to be voted on," Jimmy reminded him. "If it passes by voice vote, then we cast a confidence vote by ballot."

"Well, you might as well get the paper and pencils ready," Cory said.

Jimmy fished some out of an old cabinet. "Three-fourths of eleven would be just over eight. Eight."

"No!" Cory said, "Not eight! Eight would not be three-fourths. You'd have to have nine votes to really have three-fourths."

"Nine would be more than three-fourths," Jimmy said. "In fact, nine would be exactly three-fourths of twelve."

"Yeah, but eight is less than three-fourths of eleven, so you gotta have nine!"

I wondered who he had in his pocket besides Toby, if he had Toby. "I agree," I said. "A simple majority, six of us, have to vote to have the confidence ballot, and then nine would have to vote in favor for me to stay as president."

Cory clapped and rubbed his hands together. "Let's get on with it. Call for the question."

My heart sank when Cory, Bugsy, Toby, Jack, Matt, and Kyle voted for having the confidence ballot. Some of those didn't surprise me, but others did. I knew, as Cory had said earlier, that Jack didn't know what he was voting for or against. That was one of the prices we paid to be fair.

"Pass out the ballots and the pencils," I told Jimmy glumly. "Write yes if you want me to stay president of the club and no if you don't want me to stay president of the club."

"What do you mean, Dallas?" Jack asked. "You are president of our club."

"If you want me to stay as president, write yes. If you don't, write no."

"I'll write yes!" Jack said.

"Well, you don't have to tell everybody!" Cory said.

"Just vote, please," I said. "Turn the ballots in to Jimmy, and he'll count 'em."

"I want to check the count," Cory said.

"Fair enough."

The guys all wrote on their ballots, folded them, and turned them in. All but Jack. He didn't fold his. He held it up for all to see.

"Yes!" he shouted.

That, at least, was a relief.

Jimmy and Cory counted the other nine ballots. "No, yes, yes, yes, yes, yes, no, yes, yes," Jimmy said. "With Jack's yes, that's eight yesses."

"Yeah!" Cory shouted. "You're out! You didn't get nine!"

"I didn't vote," I said quietly.

"That's too bad," Cory said. "You abstained! You can't go back and vote now just because it didn't turn out the way you hoped."

"You have a short memory, Cory," I said. "I can't vote except to break ties, remember? This is a tie. There are not enough votes to push me out or enough to keep me in, so the chair has to vote. Right?"

He nodded miserably. "Well, I tried," he said.

"I'll tell you what I'll do," I said. "I'll vote no if you'll run against me in a new election."

"When?"

"Right now."

"Deal!"

10

Facing Fast Frank

What made me feel so great was that obviously only two of the six people who voted for having a confidence ballot voted against me. That meant that the other four had wanted a confidence vote just so they could encourage me with their yes votes. That made me feel confident that I could easily outpoint Cory in a head to head vote for president. So, I voted no on my own confidence vote and was officially out of office as president of the Baker Street Sports Club.

Jimmy had to take over the meeting as secretary, and he opened the floor for nominations for president. Toby nominated Cory. Jack nominated me. The vote was by secret ballot. I won 9-2 and could assume only that Toby and Cory voted against me. I was happy, but I couldn't smile. I hated having someone, or some two, against me like that. Cory wouldn't look at me. He just dumped his equipment and left.

"No hard feelings," he called over his shoulder.

I didn't know what to think about that. It was pretty nice, I decided, if I could believe he meant it.

Jimmy, Bugsy, and Toby stayed around talking and tossing a ball with me. One by one they had to go home, and when my mother rang the bell outside the back door, only Toby was left.

"Uh, Dallas?" he said. "Can we talk a minute?"

I shrugged. "Sure."

"I just wanted you to know that I thought what Cory did to you today was rotten."

"What he did to me?"

"Yeah, you know, this vote of confidence, wanting to be the new president, all that."

"You thought that was rotten?"

"Yeah."

"How come you seconded his motion then?"

"Because I thought nobody would vote for it but him. I was scared when he got two votes, and I felt bad that you had to vote to break the tie."

"Yeah, but it worked out, and I appreciate knowing you were on my side. I kinda thought you were the other one voting against me."

"That's what I'm kinda worried about now, Dallas. Who was the other no vote? Whoever it was must have voted for Cory for president, too. That could be trouble."

"Maybe it was Jack, and he didn't know what he was doing."

"Nah. We know for sure that on the confidence vote he was for you all the way."

"That's true. Well, Tob', ya know what? I'm not going to give it a second thought. I went from thinking nobody liked me anymore—except Jimmy—to knowing that everybody—or most everybody—is for me and was happy to prove it. I'm gonna just do the best job I know how from here on, and I'm gonna say it was a person's right to vote for whoever he wanted."

Toby moved toward our back porch and sat heavily on the steps. "I don't wanna keep you from your dinner, Dallas, but I did want to talk to you about something else."

"Sure. Just a minute, and I'll see if dinner's ready or if I'm only supposed to help with something."

I ran inside. "Mom, what do you need?"

"Dallas," she said, "dinner will be ready in about twenty-five minutes. I'd appreciate it if you could watch Jennifer while Amy is setting the table."

"Sure, Mom, but Toby wants to talk to me about something serious, and I might get a chance to talk to him about God."

"OK, I'll pray for you, and I'll tell Jenny to play out near the barn where you can see her but not have to worry about her. If you're not ready for dinner in twenty-five minutes, just send Jennifer in, and I'll understand."

"Thanks, Mom."

Jennifer ran out behind me, chanting, "I get to play by the barn, and you have to watch me!"

"What did you want to talk to me about, Tob'?" I said, sitting two steps below him.

"I just wanted to tell you I thought you acted pretty good about this whole thing. Cory was bein' a jerk all day, but you stayed pretty cool."

"Not as cool as I wanted to. But thanks for noticing that I was trying."

"That's just it, Dallas, you're always trying. How do you do it? I'm always blowing my stack."

"I need a lot of help," I said.

"From who?"

"I know this sounds strange, but from God."

"How do you get Him to help you?"

"By praying. I try to read the Bible everyday too. I also go to church every Sunday."

"So does Cory, doesn't he?"

What was I supposed to say? Several from the Baker Street Sports Club went to church with me, and a few of them had become Christians. We had asked Toby to come with us a few times, but he had never said yes. We quit asking. "Well, uh, yes, he does."

"So does he read his Bible and ask God to help him stay cool, too?"

"I don't know. He can. He should."

"Well, either he doesn't or God doesn't answer Him, because he sure doesn't act like you do. He doesn't act like Jimmy does either. I don't get it."

I was silently praying to know what to say. I don't know if God gave me the idea or not, but I suddenly got one. "Why don't you ask Cory?" I said. "Tell him just what you told me."

"I don't know about that," Toby said. "See, I was gonna tell him that I was pretty interested in church and the Bible and all that until I saw how he was acting."

We sat silent for a while. "Maybe he needs to hear that," I said.

"If you say so," he said.

"Don't tell him I said so," I said.

"OK."

"And listen, Toby, if you don't get the answers you need, come back to me, all right?"

He nodded and headed for his bike.

The next evening we were so busy and so nervous about facing Beattie's and Frank Tibbitts that I didn't even have a chance to ask Cory or Toby if they had talked. Both were unusually quiet. In fact, Cory didn't say anything. During batting practice he was terrible. During infield practice, he could hardly catch anything. And when he threw, nobody knew where the ball would wind up.

Unfortunately, that carried over into the game. Frank Tibbitts was much too much for us, and we got started on the wrong foot when Cory, our best contact hitter, the lead-off man who hardly ever struck out, struck out on three pitches. My first two times up I struck out too. I could hardly see the ball, it came in so fast. Tibbitts also had a slow hook that threw us off.

At least I was pitching OK. I gave up two unearned runs on three errors, two by Cory. Strangely, though, no matter what Cory did wrong he didn't throw his bat or yell at the umpire or the opponents or even at his teammates. In fact, he encouraged us and told us to stay in the game. We got back into it in the top of the last inning when the Beattie's coach switched Tibbitts with his left fielder. Tibbitts had allowed just a single (mine) and two doubles (Toby's and Jack's).

The new pitcher was a lefty with good control but no speed. It was like batting practice. Matt flied out deep to center, and Brent was out trying to stretch a double into a triple. Believe me, we thought a lot about that later. Brent and Jimmy hit back to back home-runs almost to the same spot over the left field fence. We had been on the brink of a loss, down by two with two out and nobody on, and we had tied the game in the top of the last inning.

Knowing that I would be facing Tibbitts to lead off the bottom of the inning, I wanted a lead in the worst way. I intercepted Andy before he left the on-deck circle. "I'm gonna have Kyle hit for you," I said. "He's smaller and maybe can draw a walk. Cory is due to get wood on the ball."

Andy turned without a word and trudged to the bench. Kyle walked on six pitches, then stole second. Cory struck out for the third time. Again he didn't get angry. He just hustled out to second and talked it up, urging me to stay sharp. I had had pretty good luck with Tibbitts, getting him twice on hard grounders to third.

This time he ripped one down the first base line between Jack and the bag, and it rolled all the way to the fence. By the time Kyle caught up with it and flung it to the cut-off man (Cory), Tibbitts was streaking for third. Cory spun and fired the ball to Toby, about chest high. Tibbitts was already into his slide, and in his hurry to get the tag down, Toby moved his glove before he caught the ball. It glanced off his glove and over his head. Suddenly, almost before it had begun, the last inning was over. Tibbitts scored, and we had lost 3-2.

The big right-hander was the first to congratulate me on a well pitched game.

"You were too much for us today," I said. Over his shoulder I saw Cory telling Toby not to worry about that last error. We shook hands all around and left the field to a nice ovation. Andy had already left.

I thought Cory would feel terrible about his part in the loss, but except for being a little quiet, he seemed all right. "I'd sure like to play them again," he said back at the shed.

"Me too," I said. "See ya, Cory."

"Uh, no, O'Neil. I need to talk to you, OK?"

"Sure. What's up?"

"Can we wait till everybody else is gone?"

I nodded. "Why not?"

11

The Disappearance

Cory's story was amazing. He said Toby had come to him that morning with all kinds of questions about God and Jesus and church and the Bible, and when Cory tried to answer them, Toby kept asking why "all that stuff" hadn't seemed to make any difference in Cory's life.

"I felt so bad, I couldn't believe it, Dallas. I mean, crabbing at you for being bossy is one thing because I know you'll forgive me. And even falling back to my old personality once in a while where I get selfish and smart alecky, like when I tried to take over the club, that was just me bein' stupid. I knew I didn't have a chance. To tell you the truth, I have no idea who else voted with me. I thought it might have been Toby because he seconded my motion, but he told me he didn't.

"Anyway, when I found out that the way I was acting was making somebody think that being a Christian didn't really make any difference, that's when I realized how bad off I was. You know I haven't been coming to church lately."

"I know."

"Well, I quit reading my Bible too. And I quit praying. And I quit telling other people about Christ. Pretty soon it seemed I was right back where I started from."

"You weren't really. You were still a Christian, but you weren't letting God control your life."

"That's for sure. Anyway, I felt so bad about Toby that I apologized to him. I invited him to church too, but he said he's not ready for that yet. He wants to watch me some more and see if I've really changed. He told me he thought I owed you an apology too, for the way I've been treating you. I prayed about it later, and I remembered how nice you've been to me, how you stuck with me when I was mean, and how you prayed for me and got me to come to church. If it wasn't for you, I wouldn't even be a Christian. So, I'm sorry, Dallas. I know I've really been bad to you."

"That's all right."

"No, it isn't."

"I mean I forgive you," I said.

Cory was embarrassed and almost crying.

So was I. I was glad when he ran to his bike and pedaled off. We didn't say anything more. We just waved at each other. I wanted to tell him he still owed Jimmy an apology, but I figured Cory had come far enough in one day.

That's why I was shocked and immediately suspected Cory the next morning when the county sheriff's police showed up at my house. My parents were in town buying shoes for my sisters, and I was home alone. Two officers, an older one who called himself Sergeant Mills and a young one named Phillips, carried a huge cardboard box. They asked to speak to my parents.

"No one's here but me," I said. "What's up?"

"Son, I'd like to see your baseball shoes," Sergeant Mills said.

"My baseball shoes? Sure! What for?"

"Just let me see them, please."

"Follow me," I said. I led them to the shed where I opened the old wood munitions box my dad gave us for our shoes and other equipment. "Let me see here," I said, riffling through the pile of shoes.

"You got a lot of brothers?" Phillips asked, noticing the many varieties and sizes of baseball shoes.

"No, the whole team keeps its shoes here."

The officers looked at each other and smiled as if this was their lucky day. "This is too easy," the sergeant said. "Let's start with your right shoe."

I handed it to him. From his cardboard box he hauled out a large plaster cast of a footprint with "Suspect number two, right," written on it in green. He held the shoe up to the cast. It fit perfectly. Then he held it next to the cast, bottom up. The brand name on the shoe appeared in reverse in the plaster.

I raised my eyebrows. That was interesting, but I didn't know where they'd taken the track from or what they thought it meant. They tried several other shoes before finding a match for the cast marked "Suspect number one, right."

"Whose shoe is this?" Phillips asked.

I was proud that I knew all the guys' shoes. "Matt's," I said.

"You guys know each other pretty well, do you?"

"We're in the same sports club."

"Together yesterday?"

"Yeah, we had a game."

"How come your shoes stink?"

"I don't know," I said, taking the left one from the box. "I was sorta wonderin' that myself." I sniffed it. It smelled faintly of manure. "My best friend has a horse, and I was near it the other day, but I don't remember stepping in any, you know, anything."

"You and this Matt together last night?"

"After the game you mean?"

"No, we mean late."

"Late? No. I was in bed by ten."

"Stay home all night?"

"Yup." For some reason I started to feel guilty. My heart raced. I didn't even know what they thought I had done, yet I felt terrible. I couldn't shake the feeling that Cory was behind all this.

"Can anybody vouch for the fact that you stayed in your house all night?"

"My parents and two little sisters were here with me."

"But if you had sneaked out after midnight, would they have had to know? I mean, can they swear you didn't do that?"

"I guess they couldn't know for sure whether or not I sneaked out."

"They wouldn't know whether you got your baseball shoes on and took Matt's to him, and you both went out after midnight?"

"I didn't do that!"

"Can anybody swear you didn't?"

"I guess not, except Matt. I've never been out with Matt."

"And would you swear Matt wasn't out late last night, early this morning?"

"Course! He wasn't. At least he wasn't with me."

"That's not good enough, son. You see, suspects can't provide alibis for each other. It just wouldn't wash."

"Alibis for what? What do you think we did?"

"You want to know what I think you did?" Phillips said, taking off his hat, smoothing his hair, and putting it on again.

"Yes, I do."

"I think you and Matt went to the Calabresi place last night after midnight and played a prank on your buddy James."

"A prank?"

"A prank," Phillips said.

"It better have been a prank," Sergeant Mills said. "You'd better have hidden that horse and know right where to find him, because otherwise, you are in deep, deep trouble."

"I didn't—we didn't—"

"Be careful now, son. Horse thievery is still a felony in this county, just like cattle rustling."

"Horse thievery! You gotta be kidding! Jimmy's my best friend!"

"Dallas, listen," the sergeant said, "that horse was missing at the crack of dawn, and we took these footprints from either side of the tracks left by the horse when he left the corral. You just told us who the shoes belong to. What we want to know is why you did it, where the horse is, and whether the horse is all right."

"I don't know anything about that. I had nothing to do with any—"

"You want to be real careful now, boy, because if we have to, we'll just wait till your parents get home, then we'll arrest you as a horse thief, and you could find yourself in juvenile lockup."

Now I was scared. "You're telling me Jimmy's horse is missing and you think Matt and I took him?"

"Just tell us where he is, say it's a joke, say you were jealous because you used to have a horse, say anything, but don't make us round up this horse somewhere and charge you with an adult crime."

"I'm innocent," I said, not feeling so innocent for some reason. "Does Jimmy think I stole his horse?"

"No. He's sure you didn't. He said you used to have a horse, so you're real happy for him. That true?"

I nodded. "You got my tracks out of his corral? Because there were several of us in the corral the other day."

"There were only two sets of tracks, one on either side of the horse's tracks this morning. Will you come with us when we talk to Matt?"

"Sure."

I left a note for my parents and rode with the officers to Matt's house. Only his mother was home. "I'm sorry," she said, "Matthew is visiting his father in New York."

"When did he leave, ma'am?"

"I took him to the airport with his sister about an hour after last evening's game. Put him on the plane myself. Then I called his father's apartment three hours later and talked to Matthew. They made it safe and sound."

"Would you have a receipt for those tickets, indicating the flight times?"

She found it. Officer Phillips phoned the airline and confirmed that Matt had been on that flight, that it had left on time and reached New York a little ahead of schedule.

"Sorry to trouble you, ma'am," they told Matt's mother.

"Can you tell me what this is all about?"

"We'd rather not until we have it all figured out."

That began a day-long investigation as the officers talked to everybody in the club. Once they found that Matt had an alibi, they assumed I was telling the truth too. They decided that somebody who knew where to find those shoes had framed Matt and me and made it look like we had done it.

I felt I had to tell them about the guys who hassled Jimmy the most. Everything pointed to Cory until they discovered that his feet were too big to fit into Matt's shoes. He couldn't have done it. At least he couldn't have done it alone. He also had an alibi. His mother was sick and up all night and would have heard him leave.

As the day wore on and more and more of the guys had solid alibis, Officer Phillips began looking more closely at the tracks, especially of my shoe print. He noticed that the heel marks and the middle of the shoe made more of an indentation than the toes. "That leads me to believe that if you weren't wearing this shoe, someone with a much smaller foot was."

He had me put on the shoes and walk in soft dirt. He made a new cast that showed an entirely different sort of impression, though it was the same shoe.

It was the shock of my life when the truth came out. We were at Andy's house, and we could tell from the minute we drove up that he was guilty. He denied it and denied it, but as the officers probed and pressed him, he finally confessed. He had slipped away from home in the middle of the night and had sneaked into our shed. He took the two pairs of shoes, went to Jimmy's, while wearing my shoes led the horse out of its stall, switched to Matt's shoes and ran backwards on the

94

other side of the horse's tracks, then ran outside the corral, smacked the horse on the rear, saw it run off, then returned the shoes and went back home.

"I'm gonna tell you something, boy, and then I'm gonna ask you something," the older officer said. "First, we found that horse. We got a call about an hour ago that he was grazing in someone's backyard in Park City, about six miles from home. You're very lucky you didn't steal him or cause him to get hurt. You know horses are sometimes hit by cars, and people are badly hurt."

Andy nodded miserably.

"Second, I want you to tell me why you did it. Why did you let this boy's horse out, and why did you choose to try to pin it on the two boys you did?"

By now Andy was crying but still trying to look at me. "I was mad at him," he said, pointing. "He bats me ninth, plays me in right field, and I'm the one who never gets to take batting practice. Something always comes up. It's too hot, everybody's too tired, we always take BP in order. When a sub comes into the lineup, we don't move up in the order. I still bat last. It's not fair.

"Jimmy got all the attention for that dumb horse. Dallas gets to be the boss."

"Why take it out on Matt, too?" Officer Phillips asked.

"He was the one who got to bat sixth when Ryan couldn't play. He should have batted ninth and let us all move up. In fact, I should be leading off."

"Andy," I said, my voice thick, "you're hitting under 200."

"That's because I never get batting practice! I always get wood on the ball."

I tried to say it kindly. "You hardly ever get wood on the ball. You lead the team in strikeouts, even though you're last in times at bat."

"See? I need more batting practice."

I was about to agree with him, to apologize, to ask his forgiveness, to promise that I would follow through on my commitment to take batting practice in reverse order half the time, but Sergeant Mills interrupted.

"Son, you're going to be charged with a misdemeanor. Do you know what that is?"

Andy shook his head.

"It's not a felony. You won't go to jail. You probably won't pay a fine. I don't know what you'll get. But you will face a judge for malicious mischief, and he may require counseling."

"Malicious mischief?" Andy repeated.

"For letting that horse out. You have a problem, son. You have way over-reacted to disappointment and misunderstanding. You can't blame this boy or Matthew for your troubles. Even if they made some mistakes, nothing justifies the dangerous thing you did and the framing of others."

Andy cried hard, and Officer Phillips drove me home while Sergeant Mills spoke with Andy's parents. I sure learned a lesson that day. There were guys in the club who thought Andy should be kicked out, but I looked forward to seeing what we could do to keep him.

I wanted his forgiveness for the ways I had ignored him, and I was eager to show him that we cared about him. If he was sorry for what he had done and wanted to admit it to everyone, my plan was to show him what true friendship was all about.